THE LEGENDS OF KING ARTHUR
MERLIN, MAGIC AND DRAGONS

Dados Internacionais de Catalogação na Publicação (CIP) de acordo com ISBD

M469q   Mayhew, Tracey
       The quest for the Holy Grail / adaptado por Tracey Mayhew. – Jandira : W. Books, 2025.
       96 p. ; 12,8cm x 19,8cm. – (The legends of king Arthur)

       ISBN: 978-65-5294-169-5

       1. Literatura infantojuvenil. 2. Literatura Infantil. 3. Clássicos. 4. Literatura inglesa. 5. Lendas. 6. Folclore. 7. Mágica. 8. Cultura Popular. I. Título. II. Série.

2025-614   CDD 028.5
                                                        CDU 82-93

Elaborado por Vagner Rodolfo da Silva - CRB-8/9410
Índice para catálogo sistemático:
1. Literatura infantojuvenil 028.5
2. Literatura infantojuvenil 82-93

The Legends of King Arthur: Merlin, Magic, and Dragons
Text © Sweet Cherry Publishing Limited, 2020
Inside illustrations © Sweet Cherry Publishing Limited, 2020
Cover illustrations © Sweet Cherry Publishing Limited, 2020

Text by Tracey Mayhew
Illustrations by Mike Phillips

© 2025 edition:
Ciranda Cultural Editora e Distribuidora Ltda.

1st edition in 2025
www.cirandacultural.com.br
No part of this publication may be reproduced, stored in a retrieval
system, or transmitted in any form or by any means, electronic,
mechanical, photocopying, recording, or otherwise, without written
permission of the publisher.
This book is a work of fiction. Names, characters, places, and incidents
are either the product of the author's imagination or are used fictitiously,
and any resemblance to actual persons, living or dead, business
establishments, events, or locales is entirely coincidental.

The Legends of King Arthur

The Quest for the Holy Grail

Retold by
Tracey Mayhew

Illustrated by
Mike Phillips

W. Books

Chapter One

King Arthur led the hunting party back through the forest to Camelot. Suddenly, a flash of bright light caught his eye. 'Did you see that?' he asked, drawing his horse to a stop.

'See what, Your Majesty?' Lancelot asked.

'There was a flash of light by the river.'

Lancelot and Gawain hadn't seen anything, but they followed Arthur's gaze.

'This way,' Arthur announced, as he dismounted and walked to a path through the trees.

Quietly telling their squires to stay behind with the horses, Lancelot and Gawain followed Arthur down to the riverbank. There they found an extraordinary sight.

Ahead of them was a slab of stone that appeared to have travelled down the river. There was a sword deeply embedded in it. The sword's golden pommel reflected the sun's rays and must have been what had caught the king's eye.

'It is just like before,' Arthur murmured, approaching the weapon.

Lancelot and Gawain glanced at each other. They had heard the story of how Arthur had drawn the sword from the stone when he had been just a boy.

'Look, there's an inscription!' Arthur called back excitedly. "Many knights will try, but only the best will draw me free", Arthur read aloud. 'Surely this

sword is meant for you, Lancelot!
I know of no better knight.'

Lancelot shook his head, taking a
step back. 'No, Your Majesty. I am
not the one meant for this sword,'
he insisted. He was thinking of his
traitorous love for Queen Guinevere.

Arthur frowned. 'But you are the
bravest knight in Camelot.'

'Your Majesty, I may be brave but I
am not the best.'

Arthur seemed disappointed but
said no more. Instead, he turned to
Gawain. 'If Lancelot will not take it,
then you must try,' he said.

Gawain looked uncertain for a
moment. Then he stepped forwards,

gripped the hilt with both hands, and pulled. The sword would not move. Gawain let go. 'It seems I am not destined for this weapon either, Your Majesty.'

Arthur frowned. As they returned to their horses, he couldn't help wondering who could be worthier than his two most trusted knights.

Upon this day, this seat will be filled.

Arthur and his knights stared at the Round Table in shock. The words had appeared in its wooden surface whilst they had

been out. No one could quite believe that after so many years, the Perilous Seat would finally be filled.

Sir Ywain gazed around at his comrades, voicing the question on everyone's mind: 'So, who is this knight we have waited so long for?'

'Your Majesty, he has arrived,' Merlin announced, before Arthur could reply.

Arthur led his knights into the Great Hall. An old man and a young one of about eighteen summers were presented to him. The young man wore plain armour and had a helmet tucked under his arm, but he carried no sword or shield.

'Your Majesty,' a guard announced. 'Naciens of Corbenic and Master Galahad beg an audience with you.'

Arthur's eyes never left the young man's face. He seemed familiar somehow. Yet Arthur knew that he had never met the youth before.

'Welcome to Camelot,' he said, as the young man bowed respectfully.

Naciens said to Arthur, 'This is Galahad. He was given to me to raise in the ways of God by his grandfather, King Pelles. He is the son of Elaine of Corbenic and Sir Lancelot du Lac,' he added, his eyes landing on Lancelot.

'I thought I saw a resemblance,'

Arthur murmured as Lancelot stepped towards the young man.

'My *son*?' Lancelot asked in disbelief. He recalled the one night he had spent with Elaine when he had thought that she was Guinevere. 'How is your mother?'

'She died, sir, when I was ten summers old,' Galahad replied quietly.

Lancelot felt a pang of sadness. 'I am sorry.'

'Since then I have lived with Naciens in an abbey not far from Corbenic,' Galahad continued.

Looking around, Naciens's eyes had found the room that held the Round Table. 'Come, Galahad,' he said. Ignoring the surprised looks of Arthur and his knights, the old man walked towards the open door. Galahad dutifully followed.

It wasn't long before everyone stood at the Round Table.

'It is as I said,' Naciens announced.

Arthur had come to stand beside him, staring down at the table in surprise. The words so recently etched into its surface had changed. Now it read: *Galahad.*

Chapter Two

'But I am not a knight,' Galahad said.

'That will soon change,' Arthur declared, drawing Excalibur. 'Kneel, Galahad.'

Before kneeling, Galahad glanced at Naciens, who nodded encouragingly.

Placing Excalibur on Galahad's right shoulder, Arthur spoke the vow

pledged by every knight. Galahad repeated the words and then it was done. He was a knight.

'Arise, Sir Galahad.'

Slowly, Galahad rose. 'Thank you,' he said to Naciens. 'You have done your sacred duty by me. In time, we shall meet again.'

Taking Galahad's hand, Naciens kissed it and left.

'Now, Galahad, take your place at the table alongside your fellow knights,' Arthur said as he and the rest of the knights found their seats.

Galahad did as instructed, slowly walking towards the empty seat. As he took his place between Lancelot and

Percival, a fierce wind sprang up from nowhere. It blew through the room, causing torches in their sconces on the walls to flicker.

'What's happening?' Ywain demanded, his eyes darting around the chamber fearfully.

'Your Majesty, look!' King Bagdemagus cried, pointing to a tiny, shimmering light hovering above the table.

Arthur stared in disbelief as the light began to expand, becoming brighter and brighter, shifting and changing shape. Finally, he found himself staring at the image of a golden cup.

'The Holy Grail,' Merlin murmured in wonder.

Just as suddenly as the light had appeared, the image vanished.

'God has spoken to us,' Galahad said, making the sign of the cross over his chest.

'I saw the Grail whilst I was at Corbenic,' Lancelot said. 'King Pelles told me that it would appear in Camelot. He said that when it did, every knight would ride out to prove himself worthy of it.'

'Then let us be tested by God!' Sir Bors declared excitedly.

'I swear on my honour that come morning, I will begin my quest for this most sacred of objects!'

One by one, the other knights echoed Bors's intention. None were louder than Percival, who was always eager for adventure. Before long, most of them had left to make preparations for their journeys. Only Arthur, Lancelot, Galahad and Merlin remained.

'Galahad,' Arthur observed, 'I see you do not carry a sword.'

Galahad shook his head. 'I was raised in an abbey, Your Majesty. I had no need for a sword. God will provide one if it is needed.'

Arthur smiled, but it was directed at Lancelot. 'I believe He already has.'

Galahad frowned. 'What do you mean?'

'Come,' Arthur said, rising from his seat. 'We have something to show you.'

It didn't take long to reach the river. After tethering their horses to nearby trees, Arthur and Lancelot led Galahad to the sword. In the fading light, the golden pommel no longer shone, but the blade did. As they approached, Arthur realised that the strange glow was coming from *inside* the sword.

Galahad stepped onto the rock and looked back at his king. 'Your Majesty, you were right to bring me here. This sword has indeed been sent by God.' Reaching out, Galahad took hold of the hilt and pulled. The blade sang as it easily slipped free.

'Now all you need is a shield,' Arthur said. 'You are welcome to take any of those at Camelot.'

'I thank you for your kindness, Your Majesty, but I must refuse. God will provide me with a shield in time.'

Arthur nodded. 'As you wish.'

'When will you leave Camelot?' Lancelot asked.

'At sunrise,' Galahad replied.

'Perhaps, until then, we could get to know one another.'

Galahad smiled. 'I would like that, Father.'

As the three men mounted their horses, Arthur hoped that Lancelot had at last found what he was looking for.

Chapter Three

The following day, Galahad rode out of Camelot as the sun rose. He and Lancelot had spent most of the night getting to know each other. Both knew that there was a good chance that neither of them would return from their quests.

After several days, Galahad saw a small church through the trees. This would be the perfect place for him to rest and seek God's guidance.

As he neared, Galahad was surprised to find two warhorses

and two ponies grazing on the grass outside. He settled his horse with them before entering the chapel. Two monks greeted him. After taking Galahad's sword, they led him to a room where two Knights of the Round Table were already eating supper.

'Sir Galahad!' Sir Ywain cried happily as he came to greet him. Behind him, King Bagdemagus rose too, his food momentarily forgotten. 'Come, we have plenty.'

Galahad joined them, glad to see familiar faces. Over their meal, the three men shared their stories of how they came to be there.

'We heard that this church has a powerful shield,' Bagdemagus began. 'Only the man capable of finding the Grail can carry it unharmed. Otherwise, he will be killed or wounded within three days.'

'We have decided that Bagdemagus will try first,' Ywain continued. 'Tomorrow he will take the shield and

ride forth whilst I stay here. If he is harmed then his squire will return with the shield.'

Galahad nodded. 'If Bagdemagus is the man destined to carry that shield, then God will protect him from harm,' he said confidently.

The following day, Bagdemagus led Galahad and Ywain to a shield mounted on the wall beside the church altar. In the morning light, the shield's white surface shone brightly around the red cross painted in its centre.

Reaching up, Bagdemagus took the shield and settled it upon his arm.

'It is only for the best knight to carry,' a nearby monk said quietly.

'And there is no reason why that should not be me!' Bagdemagus declared. Then he strode from the church to his horse and set off. His squire followed.

Bagdemagus hadn't gone far when a man wearing white armour appeared on the path ahead of him, his spear at the ready. Seeing Bagdemagus, the man spurred his horse into a gallop towards him.

Bagdemagus was only too happy to meet the stranger head-on, and prove himself worthy of the shield. But the white knight's spear easily flew over the shield, embedding itself in Bagdemagus's shoulder. Bagdemagus

was thrown screaming from his saddle. He crashed to the ground.

'Come, lad, help your master,' the white knight called to the young squire, who was now drawing his own sword. 'He has made a great mistake in taking this shield, for it was never his to take.'

'What do you mean?' demanded the squire.

'This shield is meant for Sir Galahad. Take your master back to the church and let the monks heal him. Make sure that Sir Galahad is given the shield.'

As the white knight held his horse still, the squire managed to half carry, half drag Bagdemagus to his horse. Slowly, they made their way back to the church.

The monks cared for Bagdemagus, who was seriously injured. His squire offered the shield to Galahad. 'The White Knight told me that this is meant for you, sir.'

Galahad accepted the shield.

'Thank you.' To Ywain he added, 'I must leave now.'

The squire, eager to prove himself, followed Galahad. 'May I go with you, sir?'

Galahad nodded. 'What is your name?'

'Melias, sir,' the squire replied. 'And I wish to be a knight.'

'Very well, Melias,' said Galahad. 'For bringing me the shield, I will make you a knight. I pray you will be a good and noble one.'

Together, Galahad and Melias set out on their journey. They stopped only when they reached a fork in the road. There a pilgrim explained: 'Good sirs, you must choose which path you take. The path on the right will lead you to your goal easily; the one on the left will test your strength and skills. Only the best knight should go that way.'

'I will take the left path!' Melias declared. And although Galahad encouraged him to change his mind, he would not. Thus the two knights went their separate ways. Knowing that this quest was about the strength of his soul and not of his body, Galahad had chosen the path on the right.

It wasn't long before Melias reached a clearing. In the centre of the clearing stood a splendid chair with a golden crown upon it. Melias's eyes lit up at the sight. Dismounting his horse, he approached the chair and reached out to take the crown.

'Melias,' a voice said from behind him. It was Galahad. Somehow their two paths had merged again. Galahad shook his head at Melias. 'It is not wise to take something that does not belong to you.'

'But, sir,' Melias protested, 'no one else is here. If we take it, we will be rich!'

As the sun continued to gleam off of the gold and jewels of the crown, Melias could not resist. He took it. The moment he did, a mighty roar rang out. Two knights charged from the trees. Their target was Melias.

Melias hastily made the sign of the cross over his chest. But by the time he had dropped the crown in favour of

his sword, it was too late. One of the attackers cut deeply into Melias's side. The next stroke would have killed him, but it was stopped by Galahad.

Galahad felled the knight with a well-aimed blow. The other knight spun, his blade arcing towards Galahad's head. Galahad deflected it

with his shield and launched his own attack. He sliced through the knight's wrist, severing his sword hand. The battle was won.

Galahad knelt beside Melias, who was writhing on the ground. 'I know of an abbey nearby,' he said. 'The monks there will tend to your wounds.'

Upon their arrival at the abbey, three monks came to help Melias inside. Once his wound was bandaged and they had both eaten a simple meal, Galahad told the monks what had happened.

Looking at Melias, the abbot announced, 'Your pride in choosing the path on the left, and your greed in taking the crown, has proved you unworthy of this quest. You, however,' he continued, turning to Galahad, 'remained true. You even defended your friend. Go forth on your quest, most worthy knight.'

'But–' Galahad began to protest. He did not like the thought of leaving Melias.

'Go, sir,' Melias encouraged. 'It has been an honour to travel with you. I will be a better knight for having seen your example.'

So Galahad took his leave and the abbot accompanied him outside.

'Trust in God, my friend,' the abbot murmured.

'I do,' he replied. 'With all my heart.'

And with that, Galahad mounted his horse and continued his quest alone.

Chapter Four

Sir Percival had been on his quest for many weeks. At first his mind had been focussed on finding the Holy Grail. However, it wasn't long before his thoughts turned to the woman he loved. She was called Blanchefleur.

Sometimes Percival wondered what his life would have been like if he had chosen a life with Blanchefleur over a life as a knight. He had no doubt that they would have been happy together. But he also feared that a part of him would have always longed for adventure.

Spotting a river through the woods, Percival led his horse to drink. The weather was hot and after travelling for hours they were both in need of rest. Kneeling beside the river's edge, Percival removed his helmet and splashed cool water on his face.

'What do we have here, then?' a gruff voice asked.

Percival turned to find a large group of men behind him, each carrying a club or an axe. The leader of the group, a stout, bearded man with a ragged scar above his right eye, stepped forwards. 'You're trespassing on our land,' he growled.

'This land belongs to King Arthur,' Percival said.

'Is that so?' The man laughed. 'Well, that's not how we see it.' His eyes darted to Percival's horse. 'That's a fine horse you have. Give it to us along with your sword and we will let you pass through these woods safely.'

Percival laughed. 'I'm not giving you anything! This is the king's land and I–'

The man leapt towards Percival. Percival dodged a blow from his club and drew his sword as the rest of the men surrounded him. Spooked by the fighting, Percival's horse bolted into the trees.

Alone, Percival knew that he stood very little chance against so many men. He was sure he would die. Then the thunderous beating of hooves drew near. A knight whose shield Percival did not recognise came galloping towards them. His arrival sent the gang reeling in several directions at once.

It was just the chance Percival needed. He stepped into the path of one of his attackers and disarmed him easily, tossing his axe into the water.

But when Percival turned to deal with the rest of the gang, he found that they had already fallen to the unknown knight's sword, or scattered into the wood. The knight himself was gone too.

Percival did not know how to feel. He was glad to be alive, but embarrassed that he'd had to be rescued.

He growled at the man he'd disarmed. 'If I ever hear of you terrorising these woods again, I will not be so forgiving!'

The man nodded fearfully.

'Go!' Percival ordered.

The man scrambled to his feet and disappeared after the others.

At first Percival wasn't sure what he wanted most: to thank the stranger who had saved his life, or to fight him. He made up his mind as he continued his journey. Without his horse, Percival was on foot. He grew tired and sore and angry.

He wanted to *fight* the unknown knight, he decided.

Percival walked for a day without seeing another living soul. Finally, he came across a small stone house where a grey-haired lady was tending her garden. Next to it was a horse pen with a single horse grazing inside.

'Good day, my lady,' Percival greeted her. 'Have you seen a knight ride through here? He carries a white shield with a red cross upon it.'

'Indeed I have seen him, Sir Percival of Wales.'

'You know my name!'

'I know many things,' she said mysteriously. 'The knight you seek is Sir Galahad, but you are wrong to be so angry at him. Your pride was hurt because you needed his help, but pride is a sin. Let it go, and you will meet with Galahad soon. Then you and one other knight will travel with him to Castle Corbenic in the Wasteland. That is where the Holy Grail awaits. That is where you will find the lady who has your heart.'

Percival was even more surprised to hear that than he had been to hear that the knight with the white shield was young Galahad.

'Blanchefleur?' he repeated in disbelief.

The lady nodded. 'But all of this is only possible if you do not allow yourself to be distracted from your goal. You must resist all temptations. Do you understand?' Percival nodded and the lady smiled. 'Now, take my horse. Your journey will be easier with him.'

Percival thanked the lady as he mounted the horse and rode away. Far from wanting to fight Galahad now, all Percival wanted was to prove himself worthy of journeying with him to Corbenic Castle, the Grail and Blanchefleur.

❧

When the sun began to set, Percival realised how hungry he was. He had not eaten all day. Reaching a wide clearing in the forest, he brought the horse to a stop. Before him was a huge, white tent. A beautiful lady dressed in a long black cloak stood outside it, as if waiting for him.

'Good sir, I've been expecting you,' she called. 'You have ridden hard all day and must surely be hungry.'

Percival was about to ask why

she was expecting him when she disappeared inside. Percival followed. The feast he found waiting made him forget his question and his quest.

Appearing at his side, the lady offered Percival a cup of wine. 'Drink,' she encouraged.

Percival did. The taste was strong and fruity.

Taking his hand, the lady led Percival to a chair. She filled his cup again and left him to fill a golden platter with food. As he sipped his wine, Percival's head began to spin. When his host returned, he tucked into his meal, washing it all down with more wine.

When Percival had finished, the lady gazed at him through thick, dark eyelashes. 'Percival, I have never met a man like you,' she said. 'I have heard tales of your strength and bravery.' She laid her hand on his arm. 'My heart is yours. Kiss me now and I will be the happiest woman in the world!'

For just a moment, Percival allowed himself to wonder what it would be like to kiss her. But then thoughts of Blanchefleur filled his head.
He could not betray his true love!

'Forgive me, my lady.' Percival rose hurriedly from his chair. He ignored the wine that spilt from his cup as he staggered away. He was desperate to feel the cold night air on his face. Once outside, he made the sign of the cross over his chest and asked God to give him strength.

Immediately a great wind swept through the clearing, forcing Percival to his knees. It tore the pegs holding the pavilion in place from the ground, easily carrying the tent and the lady inside it away into the night.

'Dear God, forgive me,' Percival murmured, his hand shaking as he crossed himself once more.

'Rest assured, Sir Percival, you have resisted temptation. God has forgiven you.'

Looking up, Percival saw another lady. This one was dressed in the white robes of a nun.

'Who are you?' Percival asked.

'I am Dindrane. You have proved yourself worthy. Come with me, and I

shall take you to the Enchanted Ship. Its course is set for Corbenic Castle. In time, Sir Galahad and Sir Bors will join you aboard. Bring your horse. You will have need of him later.'

Dazed, Percival untied his horse and followed Dindrane to the small bay where the Enchanted Ship was moored.

Chapter Five

Eager to begin his quest, Sir Bors had ridden out of Camelot and quickly came across a small hut. There he met a hermit.

Bors introduced himself. 'I am Sir Bors de Gannis and I am on a quest for the Holy Grail.'

'The Grail is destined for Galahad,' the hermit replied, 'but you may still witness its glory.'

'How?'

Taking his arm, the hermit guided Bors inside the hut. 'Stay a few days with me and I will teach you.'

Bors stayed at the hermitage for nearly a week. During that time, he told the hermit about the mistakes he had made and sought God's forgiveness for them. When his soul was clean, the day came for Bors to leave.

The next time his journey was interrupted, it was by the agonised screams of a man. Following the sound, Bors found his younger brother, Sir Lionel, being beaten by a gang of robbers. Lionel saw Bors and reached out, pleading. 'Help me!'

Bors was about to go to his brother's aid when another scream split the air. He looked around to see a young girl being carried off on horseback by a man.

Bors was torn: should he save his brother or the maiden? His heart told him one thing, his head another.

In the end, his head won. When Bors had taken the oath of knighthood, he had promised to protect all women. He could not turn his back on this one.

Calling on God's protection for his brother, Bors spurred his horse after the maiden. It wasn't long before he caught up. Unlike Bors, the other man was no warrior. He had no weapon and his horse could sense his fear. As Bors drew alongside, the horse reared up, eyes wide. The rider and his captive were thrown to the ground. The girl scrambled away as Bors leapt from his horse, towering over the man with his sword at his throat.

'I-I'm sorry!' the man cried. 'Please let me go!'

'Only if you swear to leave this place and never return,' Bors demanded.

'I-I will!' he stammered.

'Then go.' Bors stepped back. 'If I hear you have returned, you will regret it.'

Next, Bors approached the girl. 'Have no fear, my lady,' he said reassuringly. 'You are safe now.'

'Thank you, kind sir! I don't know how I will ever repay you!'

'There is no need. Your safety is enough.'

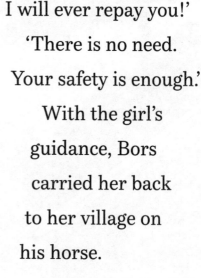

With the girl's guidance, Bors carried her back to her village on his horse.

'Father!' she cried as a man ran to meet her.

The two held each other tightly.
'I cannot thank you enough, sir,' her
father said.

Having safely delivered the maiden,
Bors hurried back to Lionel. The place
where Bors had left him was empty.
Instantly, Bors believed the worst: he
had left his brother to die.

For a long time, Bors knelt on the
grass in the silent clearing and wept.
When he finally stood and rode away,
it was without any idea where he was
going. What did it matter anymore? His
brother was dead and it was his fault.

After a day or so of travelling, Bors
reached a small village with a church.
He went inside to pray and to seek

forgiveness for Lionel's death. A monk overheard him.

'But, good sir, your brother is not dead,' he said.

At first, Bors thought he had misheard him. 'What did you say?'

'Your brother is not dead. He was brought here, and he is very much alive. Come, I shall take you to him.'

They didn't have to go far. Lionel was waiting outside when they left the church. His sword was in his hand and his bruised face was furious.

'I thought it was you, dear brother,' he muttered bitterly. 'Have you come to see what you did to me?'

'I did nothing–' Bors began.

'*You left me to die!*' Lionel shouted.

Bors hung his head guiltily. 'I'm sorry.'

Lionel took a step closer. 'You will pay for what you did,' he growled.

'I will not fight you, brother.'

'*Brother!*' Lionel scoffed. 'Some brother you are!'

Lionel raised his sword to attack Bors, but a crack of thunder split the air. A column of fire shot down from the sky, trapping Lionel inside. Through it all, Bors had made no move to draw his own sword.

Suddenly, a lady dressed in white robes appeared.

'I am Dindrane,' she told Bors. 'You have passed the test.'

'Test?' Bors echoed.

Dindrane nodded. 'By choosing to rescue that girl, and by not fighting Lionel, you have proved yourself worthy. You and Percival will witness Galahad find the Holy Grail. Come with me to the Enchanted Ship where Percival and Galahad are already waiting. The quest for the Holy Grail is almost over.'

'What about Lionel?' Bors asked, looking at his brother, still trapped in the column of flames.

'Given time, Lionel will regret his anger

towards you. For now, we must leave.'

'Forgive me, brother,' Bors murmured. Then he collected his horse and followed Dindrane out of the village.

They walked until the smell of salt and the sound of seabirds filled the air. Rounding a cliff face on a rocky path, they were greeted by the sight of a huge ship waiting in a bay. As they approached, Bors saw Galahad and Percival onboard and knew that this was the Enchanted Ship.

He followed Dindrane across the plank for whatever came next.

Chapter Six

The Enchanted Ship lived up to its name because it had no crew. It sailed itself around the coast of Britain to where the Wasteland lay wrapped in

fog. Galahad stood at the helm, silent and watchful, eager to finish his quest.

Sailing through the thick fog, the land became clearer. As they came to a stop by the shore, the knights prepared their horses and gave their thanks to Dindrane. Percival, having heaved the plank over the side of the ship, raised his hand.

'Farewell, my lady.' Then he wrapped his reins around his hand and began coaxing his horse down the plank. Once all three of them were ashore, the knights turned for one final look at the Enchanted Ship. It had already vanished, as if it had never existed.

The Wasteland was a mysterious, barren place; an endless maze of dead and dying trees, and shadowy pathways that led in circles. Its decay was tied to King Pelles's injury. Only when he was well could the land be well too.

'Are you sure this is the right way?' Percival asked for the third time.

'I am,' Galahad assured him. 'We are not far now.'

Even if he had not known the area, Galahad never feared getting lost. He knew that God would always guide him.

Sure enough, they soon came to the crumbling castle of his grandfather.

In the Great Hall, King Pelles welcomed them happily from his seat. His wounded leg was propped up on a stool as always. Behind him, Naciens was just as pleased by Galahad's safe return.

After introducing Bors and Percival, Galahad and his companions took

their seats at an empty banquet table. When it was time, the doors to the Great Hall opened and in walked the Grail procession. A hush fell over the room as everyone watched.

As always, the procession was led by a maiden carrying the Bleeding Spear. It was followed by one carrying the Silver

Tray and another carrying the Holy Grail, covered by a white cloth. Despite her hooded robes, Percival immediately recognised the Grail Maiden as Blanchefleur, the woman he loved. He wanted nothing more than to go to her but he remained seated and silent.

Next to him, Galahad seemed frozen. Just as Percival's eyes had fixed on the Grail Maiden, Galahad's eyes were fixed on the Grail. His face looked as if he were in a trance. Bors noticed too, but could only watch with Percival as the younger knight stood slowly and followed the procession into the next chamber. The door closed behind them and sound returned to the Great Hall.

'They have gone to the chapel,' Pelles explained, when Bors and Percival asked where their friend might have gone. Then the king signalled for two of his men to lift his chair. Like this, Pelles was carried and Bors, Percival and Naciens followed.

They went to the chapel and found Galahad kneeling at the altar. Golden light shone down upon his bowed head, and yet there were no windows.

Percival and Bors stood silently to one side as the Grail Maiden gently placed the Holy Grail upon the stone altar. Pelles's men lowered his chair in front of Bors. Naciens made his way to the altar, removed the white cloth and offered the Grail to Galahad.

Galahad took only one sip, but the contents of the cup seemed to fill him. He stood and turned to face those who had gathered. Already he seemed different – like calm, still water. It was as if the light that had shone down on him was now shining from inside him.

Stepping away from the altar, Galahad took the Bleeding Spear from the maiden who held it. He went to King Pelles.

'I know the pain you have suffered, Grandfather. Today it ends.' Kneeling, Galahad gently unwound the bindings from Pelles's leg and held the spear out, allowing three drops of blood to fall into the wound.

Beside Percival, Bors gasped. Pelles's wound was healing before their eyes, closing up as if it had never been there. Already, the king's face looked healthier.

'Thank you, Galahad,' King Pelles whispered, his tears falling freely.

Galahad placed a kiss upon his grandfather's forehead and thanked God for healing him. Galahad had performed many miracles during his travels, and this was his last. His quest was over. He was ready.

Those gathered saw Galahad smile contentedly before he fell to the ground. Bors rushed forward, but was stopped by Percival.

'Look!' Percival cried, pointing to the altar.

A golden light once again streamed into the room. The Holy Grail, the Silver Tray and the Bleeding Spear were drawn towards it. They rose up and disappeared, never to be seen again. Everyone watching knew that they had gone to the same place that Galahad had: Heaven.

It was a long time before anyone felt ready to leave the chapel. Bors and Percival mourned the loss of their friend, and Pelles wept for the loss of his grandson.

Afterwards, Bors stayed at Corbenic long enough to attend Galahad's funeral, and to see Percival and Blanchefleur marry. Following his marriage, Percival decided to remain at Corbenic with his wife.

'Are you sure?' Bors asked as he prepared to leave. 'You know Arthur would welcome Blanchefleur at Camelot.'

Percival nodded. 'This is where she is happiest, and I am happiest when she is.' As they embraced, Percival asked, 'What will you tell them?'

Bors smiled. 'The only thing I can: that we were witness to a great miracle. They will be telling Galahad's story for years to come, I promise you.'

And they still are.

Continue the quest with the next book in the series!

"This series opens the door to a treasure house of wonderful stories which have previously been available chiefly to older readers. We can only welcome it as a fabulous resource for all who love magical tales, and those who will come to love them."

John Matthews
Author of the Red Dragon Rising series and Arthur of Albion